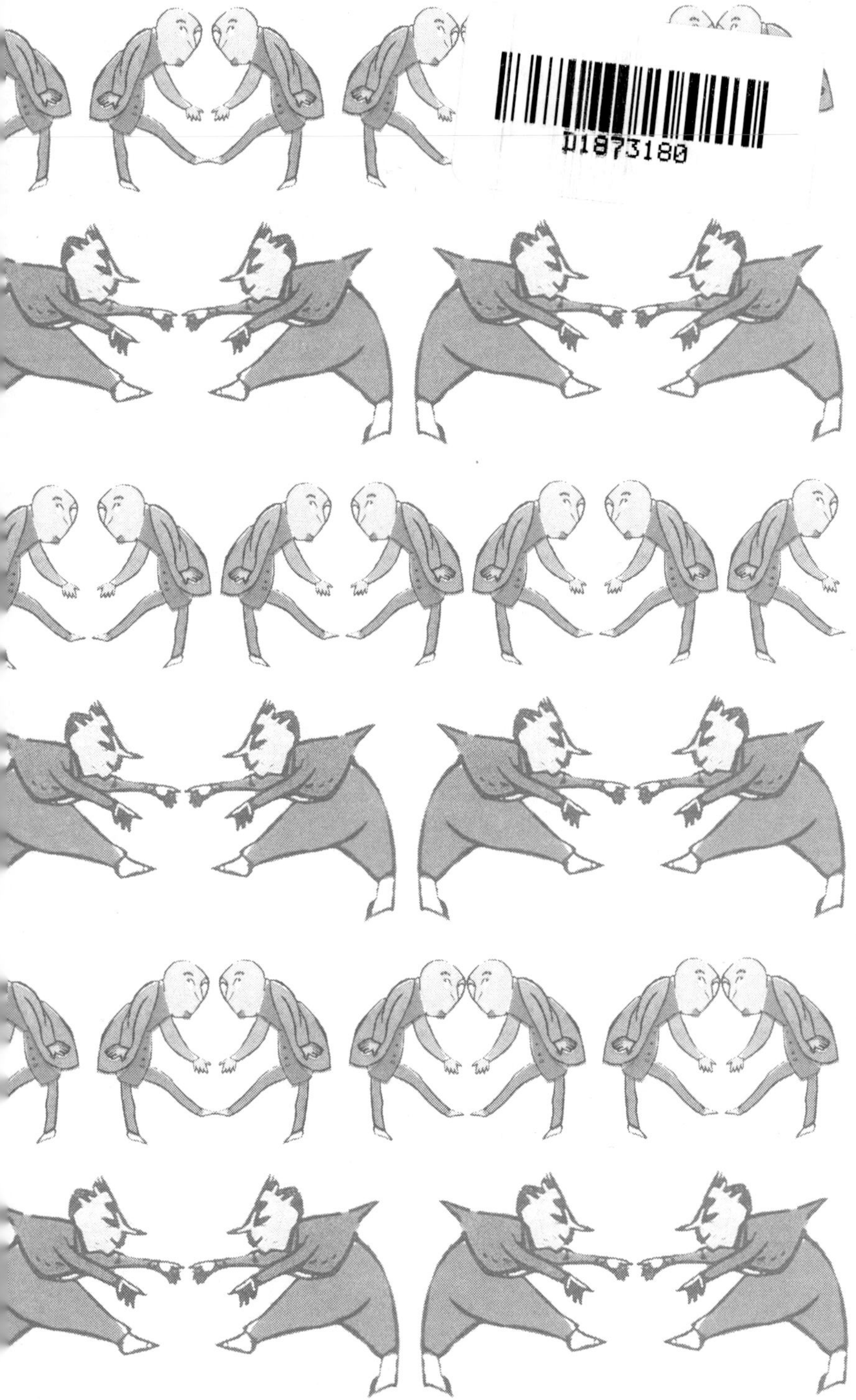

Erwin Rennert

WIRRWARR VERSE

Erwin Rennert

WIRRWARR VERSE

Ein Nonsens-Almanach
Deutsche und englische Satiren

Verlag Christian Brandstätter

„Sein Lesen also verwickelte ihn so, daß er die Nächte damit zubrachte, weiter und weiter, und die Tage sich tiefer und tiefer hineinzulesen; und so kam es vom wenigen Schlafen und vielen Lesen, daß sein Gehirn ausgetrocknet wurde, wodurch er den Verstand verlor. Er erfüllte nun seine Phantasie mit solchen Dingen, wie er sie in seinen Büchern fand, als Verzauberungen und Waffengängen, Herausforderungen, Wunden, süßem Gekose, Liebschaften, Qualen und anderem Unsinn."

Cervantes, „Don Quijote", 1. Buch, 1. Kapitel

"The hatter's remark seemed (to Alice) to have no sort of meaning in it, and yet it was certainly English."

Lewis Carroll, "Alice in Wonderland"

Inhalt

IV. A Literary Mother Goose
followed by
The Tale of the 31 Cousins (Parlez-moi d'Amour)

I. Pudelskerne, Gretchenfragen, Künstlerpost (Vita Brevis)

Love in a Gravel Pit
Festival Time

Qualvolles Dasein einer Satiriker-Gattin
(für Ruth)

Ein Satiriker in Wieren
liest der Gattin stets Satiren –
die er jeweils über Nacht
lustvoll zu Papier gebracht.
Die Geplagte sagt, es macht
ihm viel Freude, wenn sie lacht,
ja beteuert, er bezahle
ihr drei D-Mark, wenn sie strahle.
Lacht sie nicht, so nimmt er's krumm,
schilt sie undankbar und dumm.

My Zany-Zodiac-Horrorscope or Rage in Heaven

While Ram and the Twins
got hold of the Fishes,
made soup of their fins
(it tasted delicious),

the Goat and the Archer
attempted to grab
dear Virgo and march her
home to Crab.

Aquarius then poured
his water on Lion
(whom Balance ignored,
but Bull kept an eye on).

The Scorpion did linger,
reflecting, I guess,
then whetted his stinger
to show his distress.

Der Tiefpunkt

Ein Punkt von eminentem Rang,
jedoch schon seit geraumen Jahren
in leider allzu offenbarem
und letztlich stetem Niedergang,
stieß endlich ganz tief unten an,
weshalb man „Tiefpunkt“ sagen kann.
Uneigennützig er nun steht
und zeigt, ab wo es aufwärts geht.

(.)

Casting for Our New Production "The Early Bird Catches the Worm"

I shall play the Early Bird –
which leaves the Worm to you.
I'm glad to note the problems
of casting this are few.

In fact, the play requires
two actors, all in all:
your part is very crucial,
albeit rather small.

There's hardly any talking –
what is the Worm to say,
and what the Bird to answer,
so early in the day?

But then, this type of drama
is quite the latest vogue:
the unity of *action*
replacing dialogue.

Die Riesin aus der Pfalz

Eine Riesenfrau aus Bann
sah herab auf ihren Mann.

„Rainer," sprach sie (er hieß Rainer),
„du bist um zwei Köpfe kleiner.

Ich verlasse dich hiermit,
denn du bist mir zu petit.

(Falls du nochmals freist, mein Rainer,
denke dran: drei Nummern kleiner!)

Mich läßt du ab heut' in Ruhe;
freu dich, daß ich dir nichts tue."

Rainer achtete der strengen
Worte wenig – nix blieb hängen.

Also gab sie ihm Arsen
und entfloh mit Sascha Hehn.

What Did Newman Have to Do to Obtain a Red Hat?

Henry Newman
had, indeed,
to assume an-
other creed.

(Lots of Anglicans decried
his conversion as denying
their tradition, old and tried,
for another, old and trying.)

Note: the famous Anglican John Henry Newman converted to the Church of Rome (1845) and got to be cardinal (1879).

My Eight-Year-Itch*)

Instead of seven, it took eight –
everyone was waiting.
I admit I found the wait
fairly enervating.

When it came, I nearly flipped;
but my calm and clever
little woman merely quipped:
"Better late than never!"

*) "Seven year itch": a supposed tendency to infidelity after seven years of marriage. (Oxford English Dictionary)

Urlaubsende

Nun ade, Tagessuppe,
Hausplatte, Jägerspieß,
Leberknödel, Bambiteller,
Schlemm-dich-schlank-Auflauf
zu gutbürgerlichen Preisen!
Nun ade, Tiefkühlfolklore,
ihr Zeiselmauer-Buam!
Ade, Kassasturztorte mit Schlag!
Ade, Wirtinnenwunder!
Ade, Kellnerin garniert
nach Art des Hauses!
Ade, Fitness-auf-dem-Lande,
Loipenstrudel à la mode!
Servus, Urlaub! Welt, ade!

The Private Lives of Founding Fathers

Founding Fathers will, like others,
seek potential Founding Mothers.
Spotting one, they may, beguiled,
stop and found a Founding Child.

Procreation

I marvel, God, how thou hast found
by way of procreating
the human race that most astound-
ing way: of couples mating.

The couples being man and wife
(by benefit of clergy),
enacting – instruments of life –
thy sacred dramaturgy.

How Stephen C. Foster Came to Write His Delightful Song "Oh! Susanna"

I well recall Susanna,
the girl who served us many
a beer at Lackawanna
(which rhymes as well as any).

We hated Lackawanna –
the beer was pretty flat;
but she was quite a charmer,
though lately somewhat fat.

One day, while she was setting
them up, we saw her cry,
so Foster up and asks her
to state the reason why.

She told the saddest story,
how that some fellow, Sam,
had got her into trouble
and now was on the lam.

But Stephen said: "Good riddance!
you're quite a lucky maid!
Consider your dilemma,
had such a stinker stayed.

I know of lots of wenches
this bounder got with child.
Forget him, o Susanna!"
But she remained beguiled –

still claimed to "know him better",
still tried to exculpate
this Sam who had propelled her
into her blessed state.

Friend Foster wagged a finger,
then soothed the tearful miss,
by planting on her forehead
a patriarchal kiss.

He also wrote a ditty
befitting such a pro,
and called it *"Oh! Susanna"*,
this seeming apropos.

(He modified the action,
but used the damsel's name –
aware this must amount to
immortalizing same.)

Ich, das unbekannte Wesen

Ein Wesen, das nicht wußte, WER
es sei, fand diesen Zustand schwer
erträglich: die Identität
ist etwas, das uns nahegeht.
Kam jemand, es zu hinterfragen,
so wußt' es nichts von sich zu sagen,
als daß es – letztlich zweifelsfrei! –
doch immerhin vorhanden sei.

Doch ist man wer, so liegt es nah,
man hieße Puck, Caligula,
Raskolnikow, Rautendelein,
Ulysses oder Frau von Stein.
Man hieße Thatcher, hieße Gretchen
(man wäre Missis, wäre Mädchen);
man hieße Mimi, Marc Anton,
vielleicht auch Hure Babylon.

(Man sieht, das unbekannte Wesen
war außerordentlich belesen!)

Und fehlt der Name, fehlt das Um
und Auf für ein Spezifikum:
ein kleiner Zipfel Raum und Zeit
verharrt in Unverbindlichkeit.

Heißt man nicht Heidi, Messalina,
nicht Yoko Ono, Palestrina,
nicht Klimt und auch nicht Mickymaus,
weicht man in die Semantik aus –
und rätselt mit der Welt: Worin
liegt die Bedeutung von „Ich bin"?
Man *ist* in kleinen Schüben nur –
von Dauerzustand keine Spur.
Nach der Grammatik klaren Thesen
ist man, entsprechend, auch *gewesen;*
und *wird* sogar (mit etwas Schwein,
so man uns läßt) auch morgen *sein* . . .
Doch *wer* man ist (und wenn, wozu),
das war und ist und bleibt tabu.

Ein kunstsinniger Tüncher

Ein Tüncher aus Gent an der Schelde
fälscht laufend berühmte Gemälde.
Hat er heut' keinen Schiele
oder Klimt in der Diele,
so „besorgt" er sie wohlfeil in Bälde.

Verlorenes Ich im Kursalon

(für Gottfried Benn)

Es glitzert die Glatze,
es schmitzelt das Aug',
es süchtelt die Schmatze,
es rundet der Saug;

es wogen die Kinne,
es kräuselt das Hirn,
es schillern die Sinne,
es runzelt die Stirn;

es wackeln die Ohren,
es süßelt der Zahn:
es tritt mein *verloren –*
es Ich auf den Plan . . .

Schon rötelt die Wange,
es lüstelt der Mund –
und folget dem Drange
und frißt sich gesund.

Festival Time

Rudolf Serkin
downs a gherkin,
then does well
by Ravel.

Isaac Stern
takes his turn,
shares a herring
with Henryk Szeryng.

Josef Krips
spills his chips,
throws a fit
in the pit.

Piltdown Jack & Piltdown Jill*) or Love in a Gravel Pit

Piltdown Jack meets Piltdown Jill –
palaeontologic thrill.
Piltdown Jill beds Piltdown Jack
(in a gravel pit, alack!).

*) A rather primitive couple, faking very early existence at Piltdown, Sussex (based on lowbrow skull fragments uncovered in a local gravel pit).

Romeo Cuts Names into Trees or Parlez-moi d'amour

The girl who makes my day
is J-U-L-I-A.
She's prettier, I guess,
than D-O-R-I-S;
and brainy, rating well
above J-I-L-L.
Though of a lower age
than E-D-I-T-H,
she's more maternal than
E-I-L-E-E-N.
(Her folks have, by the by,
more M-O-N-E-Y.)

Keeping Her Chin Up (Face-Lifting)

I see her chin is kept up high,
whatever state she's in,
but wonder who would pay (and why)
the upkeep of her chin?

For keeping chins up isn't cheap;
and there are few adept
and prosperous enough to keep
a chin like her's upkept.

Dichters Dilemma

Ich habe viel zu viel Papier gestohlen,
womit soll ich das alles nun beschmieren –
woher den Stoff für die Gedichte holen,
damit geneigte Leser zu sekkieren?

Ich mag nicht mehr die alten Strophen leiern,
doch woher neue nehmen, womit läßt
Gedankenblässe sich so wohl verschleiern,
wie mit dem Daktylus, dem Anapäst?

Auch Reimen ist nicht, was es einmal war:
nach Vogelweide, Rilke, Busch und Benn,
zitiert, was brauchbar ist, zu offenbar
Extravaganzen dieser Gentlemen.

Besonders aber fehlen mir Ideen,
die meisten guten wurden längst benützt –
ich würde auch die dümmsten nicht
verschmähen,
doch sind auch sie durch Copyright geschützt.

Das Lied vom Samenspender*)

Er spendet Samen, wo er kann –
kommt ihm ein Mensch entgegen,
und ist's ein Weib und Not am Mann,
schon folgt der Samensegen.

Er reflektiert auf kein Labor
für solcherlei Bescherung,
ein Bett genügt (und ist recht vor-
teilhaft für die Vermehrung).

Er braucht auch keine Konzession,
Patente und Lizenzen –
ein Bett, ein Weib genügen schon
für seine Kompetenzen.

*) Melodie: „Der Plumpsack geht rum".

Having my Cake and Eating It

I see no problem, I confess:
I *eat* the cake I have, I guess;
reversely, in the most concrete
of terms, I *have* the cake I eat.
(When it's gone, my cheerful mother
never fails to bake another.)

Man with Beard

The man with beard
was widely feared:
the people feared him –
ergo sheared him.

A lesson this,
what wrath do brave
the men who miss
their daily shave.

Umweltalarm: Oder-Neisse

Ein Mann, der immer traurig war,
wußt' nicht, was dies bedeute:
es ging nicht an, das wußt' er zwar,
daß man sich immer freute;

doch daß die Tage grau in grau
verliefen, wußte er genau
sowenig zu erklären wie
die Leibnizsche Philosophie.

Von dieser hieß es, sie verheiße,
daß immer alles bestens sei;
doch hielt er dies für Schwärmerei:
Es floß und fließt beständig Scheiße
hinab die Maas und/oder Neisse.

Godot and His Fabulous Troupe

Some say he was invented –
a funny thought, or is it,
for people discontented-
ly waiting for his visit.

Myself, I think there should be,
nay, *must* be a Godot:
for were there not, why should we
be always waiting so?

If presently unable
to come, he some day may,
that Grand Old Man of fable
(and, lately, of a play).

Well, anyway, we waited,
but also had a go
at saying how we hated
this waiting for Godot.

When Beckett heard it mentioned,
he mumbled: "Lucky me!
This story suits my penchant
for trenchant comedy."

So all of us got famous –
Godot and Sam and us;
the audiences acclaim us,
'cause we're so fabulous.

Tourism: Pay-As-You-Go

The Duchess of Kent
paid-as-she-went:
she scattered pennies
all over Venice,
got back to Kent
without a cent.

BESTSELLER

Ein Roman,
der in Japan
spielte
und Erfolg erzielte,
auch in jedem anderen Land
allerhöchst im Kurse stand
(miserabel übersetzt
las der Gute sich sogar
auf aztekisch wunderbar),
von den Kritikern geschätzt
und – Verleger freut das mächtig –
auch schon Prix Goncourt*)-verdächtig,
von den Lehrern unentwegt
abgehandelt und zerlegt,
umgedeutet nach Belieben,
im Methodenstreit zerrieben,
mit Signifikanz gestopft,
auf Strukturen abgeklopft,
von Banausen kommentiert,
immer öfter falsch zitiert . . .
seinen Lesern endlich tat
kund in einem Inserat:

„Sprachgewaltig aber müd,
suche ich alsbald zwecks steten
Aufenthalts am Pole (süd)
Zimmer bei Analphabeten."

*) ansehnlicher französischer Literaturpreis. – *„Rennert wünschte sich einen Prix Goncourt, bekam aber keinen."*

LIBI-DO'S, LIBI-DON'TS

I know few who will refuse
paying heed to libi-do's,
but a lot of folks who won't
heed a single libi-don't.

"Don't change horses in mid-stream."
– A. Lincoln (1864)

What Activities Should We NOT Undertake in the Middle of the Stream?

In the Middle of the Stream,
Lincoln said (and, it would seem,
rightly), our only course is
to Abstain From Changing Horses.

And we should Not Rock the Boat,
(should we notice one afloat),
lest it be the Ship of State
which we thusly agitate.

Casual Sex

When I am tired, I am prone
to go to bed – and this alone,
much hoping nothing will encumber
my hours of repose and slumber.

And yet I'm subject, now and then,
to forces quite beyond my ken:
I sleep, I dream, I toss and shake,
sit up – alone, asweat, awake.

I wonder then if someone crept
into my bed the while I slept;
and, were it so, I'm also bent
on learning his or her intent.

Would whosoever be it care
to know 'tis I whose bed they share?
And – tit for tat – give me a clue
on who they are and what we do?

II. Zahn der Zeit (und andere Zähne)

Jack the Ripper on his Day off

Der Originalgaraus

Garaus begibt sich eines Herbstes
vor seines Onkels Haus und hofft,
daß dieser stirbt; denn schon gar oft
sprach er zum Neffen: „Sterb' ich, erbst es."

Garaus, geschickt, bei Kerzenschein,
dringt ins ersehnte Häuschen ein,
beschleicht den lieben Alten leise
und – handelt, konsequenterweise.

Seither spricht man in Erbschaftssachen
von „jemandem den *Garaus* machen",
was heißen will: man geht bei reichen
Verwandten über deren Leichen.

Burying the Hatchet

Sick of feuding, I conceived
that the hatchet might be buried;
grabbing it, my mind relieved,
to mine enemy I hurried.

There arrived, I thought I made him
see my line of thinking, and,
showing him the hatchet, bade him
let me bury it as planned.

He agreed, but soon repented
this, and asked me to refrain,
when he realized I had meant it
to be buried in his brain.

Jack the Ripper on his Day off
or Having a Ripping Good Time

Jack the Ripper, at his best,
needed very little rest;
he was rarely of a mind
to escape the daily grind.

When, however, he at length
felt he must restore his strength,
he would manage this by way
of a walking holiday.

One such time, he happened, hiking,
on a female to his liking,
and, in an attempt to please,
stopped a bit to bat the breeze.

Happily, she proved to be
very good at repartee,
never really, by and by,
seeming lost for a reply.

Jack experienced some elation
at this form of recreation:
just to banter, place a pun,
seemed to him a lot of fun.

Suddenly he had a galling
recollection of his calling –
of the craft by which he came
to enjoy a certain fame.

"Jack the Ripper, you are slipping!
Mustn't disappoint the folks!"
But for once he found it ripping
simply to be trading jokes.

The Pamphleteer

The pamphleteer
felt little cheer:
he knew his copy
was so sloppy,
and sure as hell
it wouldn't sell.
Its thesis, too,
was hardly new;
besides, he found
it quite unsound
(and, even more,
a grisly bore).
He wondered why
a soul should buy,
for honest cash,
such balderdash!

The pamphleteer
felt fairly queer –
familiar plight
to folks who write
(though most are wont
to be less ruth-
less in confront-
ing ugly truth).

(to be sung to the tune of "Rum and Coca-Cola")

Split Second Timing

I know a man who likes to split
his seconds into slivers. It
appears, he does it with a view
to gaining time. He saves it too:
each night, the hugest sliver stack
bears witness to his special knack.

JEDWEDER

Es kennt ein jeder doch
das alte WEDER – NOCH;
doch weiß vielleicht nicht jedes
sein WEDER, WEDE, WEDES.

FEIN(D)KOST

(aus: *Gesünder leben für Kannibalen*)

Will man der Mangelkrankheit wehren
(genannt auch Avitaminose:
an ihr litt früher der Matrose),
so muß man einen Feind verzehren.
Der Feind ist reich an Vitaminen
(so sagen Ärzte – glaube ihnen!),
ist eisenhaltig auch und, wahrhaft,
als Eiweißspender äußerst nahrhaft.
Man gibt ihn gerne als Pastete
mit Apfelkren und roter Bete;
als Leckerbissen, mariné,
mit pommes de terre à l'eau salée.
Im Sommer schmeckt er wunderbar
gekühlt, auf Toast, mit sauce tartare.
Doch eignet er sich, entre nous,
auch für's bescheidene Ragout,
ersetzt das fade Tofu auch
im Eintopf für den Hausgebrauch.
Gelernte Kannibalen pflegen
ihn für den Winter einzulegen
(dazu bedarf es aber, falls es
versucht wird, auch des Pökelsalzes).
Verpackt als „Vollwertfeindesgrütze –
die tägliche Verdauungsstütze"
bekommt man ihn – als dernier cri –
in jeder guten Drogerie.
Die Apotheken führen ihn
als Herz- und Kreislaufmedizin

(rezeptepflichtig nach dem Willen
der Ärzte) auch in Form von Pillen,
in Fläschchen auch, als Destillat,
im Sack, als Pulverpräparat,
als Salbe noch, im kleinen Tiegel,
versehen mit dem Gütesiegel.
Am besten freilich kommt er*) frisch
auf den gepflegten Mittagstisch.

*) Mit „er“ und „ihn“ ist, wie es scheint,
vom Autor stets „der Feind“ gemeint;
den er nicht näher definiert
(er wollte nämlich keinen kränken).
Vermutungen sind deplaciert:
es darf sich jeder *seinen* denken.

THE PRESBYTER'S TALE

In my youth I went chasing
skirts, thus debasing
my subsequent calling
in a manner appalling.

Well was I known
quite to disown
the things of the spirit,
or anything near it.

Potency spent,
I did me repent,
escaping the mesh
of sins of the flesh.

Now safe, I recall
the depth of my fall,
and shudder to think
of those on the brink.

I deeply reflect
on sins I detect –
and I certainly spot
a hell of a lot!

THE SAMURAI

Sitting on
a biggish towel
(time anon
to disembowel),
the samurai
heaved a sigh:
hara-kiri
seemed so dreary.

Was it fitting,
was it chummy,
to be slitting
such a tummy?

For the bother,
he'd spill lots
rather *other*
people's guts.

Sure. Yet, still,
he'd had an omen
boding ill
for *his* abdomen . . .

LIED DER VEREINSPOLIZEI*)

Ferne Glocken läuten leise
einem ganz intimen Kreise.

Höre, Kreis, besagtes Läuten!
Frage dich, was soll's bedeuten?

Lausche, Kreis, dem leisen Schritte –
einer tritt in deine Mitte.

Einer löst dich leise auf:
unintimer Weltenlauf.

*) Melodie: „Junge, was machst du da?"

„Feind hört mit“

Der Feind hört mit, doch fragt sich was
er mithört und wozu –
wir schwätzen ohne Unterlaß
und rauben ihm die Ruh’.

Ermüden muß der viele Mist
den Armen, und verstören –
doch die Funktion des Feindes ist
nunmal, uns zuzuhören.

(Melodie: „Schwer, langweilig ist mir mein Zeit“ – *Des Knaben Wunderhorn*)

Geschichtsunterricht: Die Dicke Liga

Die Dicke Liga war entstanden.
Hoch loderte die Hoffnung derer,
die darin viel zu hoffen fanden;
sie hatte etliche Verehrer.

Doch manchem schien sie allzu dicklich –
und dieses machte sie zunichte:
Sie ward – o Schicksal unerquicklich! –
ein dickes Opfer der Geschichte.

Man zeigt wieder Knie

Man zeigt heuer wieder Knie
und, als Zubehör, die -kehlen;
und auch schöne Schenkel hie
und da – auch sie
sollen nicht fehlen.
Doch hat’s damit nicht sein Bewenden:
Man zeigt auch wieder gerne Lenden;
und dazu, letztlich, gegen Langeweile,
auch wieder einprägsame Hinterteile.

RESEARCH INTO AN UNLITERARY FRENCH BROTHEL (Summary of Findings)

These girls, it seems, had never heard
much mention made of the Absurd;
I found *The Stranger* rang no bell,
except as he had things to sell
(or happened to be looking for
some recreation with a whore).
My questions on the drama of
Jarry, Artaud, and Adamov,
on Dada tenets, cubist style,
drew but an unbelieving smile.
They had no notion of Genet;
and apprehended *La Nausée* –
so one explained in accents mild –
as meaning that one was with child.
This said, it could not be expected
they'd offer useful views on Beckett.

(Godot had never let them wait
for folks with whom to fornicate,
but this inspired little cheer.)

From the above it would appear
that whores derive their innocence
from literary abstinence.
Without much fussing or ado
they face their Anguished Choice or two
(though none accepts, or will admit,
that Kierkegaard invented it).
They do not feel a pressing need
to sip the heady stuff of Gide,
have never known, and never missed,
the joys of his *Immoralist.*

As for their big and pleasant Madame,
she didn't know Camus from Adam.

Confessions of a Professional Go-Between Quite Ignorant of his Clients' Identity

I go between, but know not who
requires me to do it.
Quite early in the game, I do
admit, I wished I knew it.

Since then I've come to execute
my duty, as I see it:
as go-between, who must commute
'twixt whosoever be it.

Mit Vorurteilen leben

Ich liebe meine kleinen Vorurteile;
speziell seit ich in reifen Jahren bin,
sind sie ein Mittel gegen Langeweile
und Stütze für den Orientierungssinn.

Ich blättere in ihnen wie in Heften
voll Photos aus der guten alten Zeit,
ich labe mich an ihren Zaubersäften,
gebraut aus Galle und Besinnlichkeit.

Ich will nicht, daß man sie in Frage stellt,
noch meinen Blick auf neue Kenntnis lenkt,
denn aus dem ersten Zweifel schon erhellt
ein weiterer, an dem das Ganze hängt.

Und dieses darf ich nimmermehr gefährden:
Gewißheit, klare Linien, eine Sicht
der Dinge, wie sie waren, sind und werden,
besehen, wie man sagt, bei rechtem Licht.

Erleichterung ist sicher angebracht,
gelingt es mir, mein Weltbild zu erhalten –
vorurteilslos darüber nachgedacht,
laß ich doch lieber Vorurteile walten!

HOMO TECHNICUS TRYING TO RAISE A LAUGH
(Mission Report)

Though we used some expert staff,
proper gear, the latest winches,
all we did was raise the laugh
by some negligible inches.

So we got the biggest crane,
which, however – it's a bitter
fact I cannot quite explain –,
never even raised a titter!

JUNGE EUMENIDEN

Auf Anschluß hofften im Gesträuch
zwei junge Eumeniden.
Sie baten uns, sie baten euch,
sie gaben keinen Frieden.

Sie baten Mann, sie baten Weib –
war keines, das sie freite.
Nun zeigen sie sich zum Zeitvertreib
von ihrer schlimmsten Seite.

USES OF TEETH

Some folks delight
in nails to bite,
to others, gnashing
teeth seems dashing;
still others find
it fun to grind
their teeth or chew
a lip or two.

Spellbound

The words I'm daily *bound to spell*
are many, and I do it well;
in fact, I take a certain measure
of pride in it, and even pleasure.
Each Sunday, between two and three,
I join a giant spelling-bee,*)
in which to demonstrate at will
my wondrous orthographic skill.
The other day, I really sent
them sprawling with "grandiloquent"
(which some contestants, quite at sea,
preferred to spell with "k" and "v").
And I've won firsts for spelling "Whig",
"flamboyancy" and "whirligig".

*) spelling-bee: a spelling contest (for people tired of watching CNN) in which contestants are eliminated as soon as they misspell a word. (They can then return to watching CNN.)

Latter Days: Opium for the Masses

Polyvinyl chloride flowing
through the richly Stygian night –
dainty little feet are toeing
lines converging out of sight.

Opiates are hoping faintly
that the masses might be near;
seedy souls are crying quaintly
over pots of brackish beer.

Itsy-bitsy worms are feeding
overtime and manage quite
(though their gums are gently bleeding)
to maintain an appetite.

Tatenbank im Himmel

Im Himmel haben sie den größten Computer,
zur Speicherung von Namen und Taten
in einer Tatenbank (mit T wie Traugott).

Wenn auf Erden ein Werk genannt wird
oder seine Folgeerscheinung
durch die Köpfe geistert,
ohne daß man wüßte, wer das gedacht,
getan, ausgeklügelt oder eingemacht,
verfaßt, verzapft, verkörpert,
verübt oder verbrochen hat,
wer eine Schnapsidee sein eigen nannte,
ehe er sie in die Missetat umsetzte –
dann flackert dort oben der Bildschirm:

/ Spyri, Johanna / / Schmidt, Schnauze /
/ Guillotin, Dr. / / Grimm, Brüder /
/ Reagan, Ronnie / / Bonsels, Waldemar /
/ Helena, schöne (Rubinstein?) /
/ ACHTUNG /§§§§§§§§/ ACHTUNG /
/ gedacht wird an / / Erwähnung finden /
/ Alm-Öhi / / Nachrüstung / / Köpferollen /
/ Holle, Frau / / Wars, Star / / Maja, Biene (?) /
/ casus belli / / Schönheit kommt
aus der Parfümerie (?) /

Dann freuen sich da droben
langvergessene Leute auf ihren Hinterbänken,
und sie bekommen ein Sternchen
in ihr Soldbuch geklebt.

Wenn einer hier unten sagt:
„Wie nützlich ist doch die Wasserstoffbombe!"
oder „Immerhin gibt es noch Sex",
dann blitzt es gleich über den Bildschirm:
„Teller, Vater der", „Miller, Vater des".

Sagt ein Arzt in Püspökladany:
„Der Patient leidet an Anämie"
oder fragt z. B. ein Pirat in Penzance:
„Wieviel Wasser verdrängt dieses Schiff?",
dann heißt es sofort:
„Anämie siehe *Blutmangel* –
Drakula, Vater des"
und „siehe *Verdrängung* –
Freud, Vater der".

Lobt einer die Schöpfung, dann respondiert
der Computer (mit einem Anflug von
Lächeln):
„Haydn und/oder Lieber Gott".

Doch ärgert sich jemand auf Erden
und fragt: „Wer hat diesen Mist gebaut?",
dann weiß der Blechtrottel nicht,
ob wir den kleinen Mist meinen
oder den großen. Dann flimmert es nur so,
und der Bildschirm wird ganz schwarz.

Best Foot Forward

Let us all concentrate
on putting our best feet forward.

Let me each morning, on rising, ask:
Which is my best foot?
Then let me put it forward.

Let our best feet
not be dragging their heels.
Let them be an example to worse feet.
Let each be a foot for the good!

That they who come after,
seeing our prints in the rock, may say:
„These were their finest feet."

Fülle des Daseins

Die Daseinsfülle nimmt mich wunder:
die Menschen werden immer runder.
Bald kugeln sie schon, statt zu wandern,
von einem üblen Ort zum andern.

Und Kinder wachsen auf und rollen
um eins, zwei Ecken und sind bald verschollen.
Und Vögel kommen immer angeflogen
und setzen sich auf unsre müden Füße
(von fernen Müttern bringen sie die Grüße).
Ein Leitartikler schreibt verlogen.

Eine gefährliche Baronin

(Minimoritat Nr. 1)

Die Baronin Derben-Zerben
wollte den Baron beerben,
also gab sie ihm Strychnin
in den Schnaps und killte ihn;
kürte sich dann, rasch entschlossen,
einen neuen Bettgenossen.
Dieser hielt sie für erpreßbar –
also starb auch er bald, n'est-ce pas.

Die Mär von der Dame im Watt

(Minimoritat Nr. 2)

Ein reicher Reeder, wohnhaft Wanna,
haßte seine Gattin Hanna.
(Müßt' er, Gott behüte, sterben,
würde *sie* den Laden erben;
unerträglich der Gedanke
auch für seine Freundin Anke.)
Also macht' er Hanna halt
mittels Strangulierung kalt –
morgens fand man sie im Watt –
und beerbte *sie* anstatt.

III. Ein Brei kam einst zu seinem Koch . . .

gefolgt von

Spukgeschichten:
Ein Widerspruchsgeist

Ein Brei

Ein Brei kam einst
zu seinem Koch
und hämisch sprach:
„Versuch mich doch!"

Der Koch, ihm grauste,
als er so jauste.

Alter Ego

Der Ego war mit neunzig Jahren
der älteste der Janitscharen.
Was Wunder, daß zum Hochbetagten
sie alle „alter Ego" sagten.

Ein Wurfspiess

Ein Wurfspieß sucht initiativ das Weite
und freut sich schon im Stillen auf sein Ziel;
durch den Besuch, so hofft er wohl, bereite
er jenem ebenso der Freude viel.

Allein das Ziel hofft wenig von dem Gere,
winkt ab und läßt den Nahenden verstehen,
es schätze die ihm zugedachte Ehre,
doch wolle nicht an ihr zugrundegehen.

„Der Krug geht so lange zum Brunnen, bis er bricht"

Zum Brunnen ging einstmals
so lange ein Krug,
bis einer sich seiner
erbarmt' und ihn trug.

Doch täten wir solches
mit sämtlichen Krügen,
wie sollten die je noch
dem Sprichwort genügen?

Betrachtung zum Thema „Die Sonne bringt es an den Tag“

„Die Sonne bringt es an den Tag“ –
es sei denn, es ist Nacht,
was dann zur Folge haben mag,
„es“ wird an sie gebracht
(und demgemäß natürlich nicht
vom Sonnen- sondern Mondeslicht).

Symbolträchtig

So ihr trachtet nach Symbolen,
wird euch bald der Kuckuck holen –
ergo meide Jung und Alt
tunlichst den Symbolgehalt!
Hüte sich, auf irgend Zeichen
vom Konkreten abzuweichen;
fische stets und allerorten
nur nach Wörtern, nie nach Worten!

O Daseinskampf!

O Daseinskampf –
ein steter Krampf
an diesen wüsten Küsten!
Ach, wenn wir doch
aus diesem Loch
ein Loch ins Freie wüßten!

Und Bruderzwist,
wie arg du bist!
Jedoch in andern Nestern ist,
wer weiß, ein arger Schwesternzwist?

Drei Akte auf der Flucht vor ihrem Autor

Ich bin der 1. Akt
und fühle mich so nackt;
auch gibt es an mir grauen-
haft wenig anzuschauen.

Ich bin als 2. Akt
schon reichlich abgeschmackt
und trete auf der Stelle –
Teil der (b)analen Welle!

Ich bin der 3. Akt
und gänzlich abgesackt;
das kommt vom Herrn Autoren,
der hat mich totgeboren.
(Ich wollt', der Vorhang fiele
auf dieses sein Versagen;
doch läßt die „Lust am Spiele"
ihn gleich sein nächstes wagen.)

Geisterkinder: Wes Geistes Kind?

Wes Geistes Kind
die Kinder sind,
muß man die Mütter fragen.
Doch werden die es nicht geschwind
dem ersten besten sagen.

Ein Kammerdiener

Ein Kammerdiener – er war Wiener –
folgt seiner Herrschaft – einer Frau –
nach Bayern und ward Ammerdiener,
ich glaub' in Oberkammergau.

Trendwende

Ich habe alle Hände
voll mit der ollen Wende.
Wer hätte je gedacht,
was es für Mühe macht,
den Trend mit seinen zähen
Tendenzen umzudrehen!

Der Gegenstand

Tagsüber stand an einer Wand
ein kleiner lieber Gegenstand;
doch war er nachts, bis knapp vor Tag,
ein kleiner lieber Gegenlag.

(Melodie: „Was steht in diesem Winkel da?")

Fortschritt

Zum Beispiel, ein Ort mit
Abort ist ein Fortschritt.

Die Wesensfremden

Um Mitternacht, auf ihren Besen,
sieht man die kleinen fremden Wesen.
Es flattern stark die weißen Hemden
der Wesensfremden.

(Melodie: „Wir Wiener Waschweiber")

Aus einer alten Chronik

Als Quidam aus der Anstalt floh,
fand Zuflucht er beim Quidproquo.
Dann zeugten jährlich sie viermal
ein kleines schreiendes Quartal.

Fallobst

„Der Apfel fällt nicht weit vom Baum",
das lernt wohl jedes Kind;
doch weiß es auch, daß Birn' und Pflaum'
in diesem Lehrsatz minder kaum
mit inbegriffen sind?

(Melodie: "Don't sit under the apple tree
with anyone else but me")

Schnurstracks

schnur- spricht zu -stracks:
„mach keine fax'
und bleibe nur
bei deiner schnur-!
dir soll's beileibe
gut gehen – bleibe!"

-stracks aber spricht:
„ich bleibe nicht!
denn eure schwüre
kennt man, schnüre-!"

Tempus fugit

Nihil obstat jedermann,
alle können, keiner kann;
urbi orbi Freundeskreis,
alle wissen's, keiner weiß.
Ipso facto treibt's der Küster
(„carpe diem") immer wüster.

Wenn alle Stricke reissen

„Wenn alle Stricke reißen",
frägt bange mein Genick,
„so reißt doch, will das heißen,
wohl auch der Galgenstrick??"

Zahlen zählen

Neuner neunen,
Achter achten,
Sechser sechsen,
Fünfer schmachten.

Zehner zehnen,
Dreier dreien,
Einser sehnen
sich nach Zweien.

Lebenswandel

Lebenswandel?
Lebensschandel!

Sechs Lieder aus Rennerts Zitatenschatz

1. Geschwister

„Alle Menschen werden Brüder",
hieß bei Schiller es noch gestern,
doch ich glaube, um die Hälfte
eignet eher sich zu Schwestern.

2. Lied an die Übervölkerung

„Seid umschlungen, Milliarden!"
Doch es singen noch die Barden
von den Zeiten, von den Zonen,
da umschlang man bloß Millionen.

3. Der Cliquen-Song

Wie fruchtbar ist der kleinste Kreis,
wenn man ihn zu begatten weiß!

4. Mitternacht in Babylon

Die Mitternacht zieht näher schon –
und siehe, es verspricht
Belsazar sich nicht mehr davon
als höchstens ein Gedicht.
(Gott schreibt es nicht alleine,
es hilft ihm Heinrich Heine.)

5. Die Hydra

Er zählt die Häupter seiner Lieben –
und sieh, ihr fehlt kein teures Haupt!

6. Nachtgesang des Argus

„Müde bin ich, geh' zur Ruh',
schließe alle Äuglein zu."

Ein Widerspruchsgeist

Es war ein Geist dem Widerspruch verfallen –
er wohnte täglich Diskussionen bei
und merkte allsogleich bei ihnen allen,
daß keine These akzeptabel sei.

Er ließ es nie an Höflichkeit gebrechen,
ja lächelt öfters mal den Redner an,
ermuntert ihn, doch alles auszusprechen,
damit er besser widersprechen kann.

Ein gutes Argument weiß er zu schätzen,
doch kaum vernommen, folgt er seinem Triebe,
sich ihm mit Vehemenz zu widersetzen
(auf daß es nicht unwidersprochen bliebe).

Bei Goethe habe ich einmal gelesen
von einem Geist, der alles stets negiert –
dies hätte unsern Geist zu Antithesen
im positiven Sinne provoziert.

Doch kürzlich, hört man, kam auch er beinahe
um seinen Ruf, in einer Diskussion
zum Frauenpriesteramt: ob man's bejahe,
und wenn, um echten oder Gotteslohn.

Da war der Geist in seinem Elemente!
Gerüstet steigt er in das Wortgefecht;
im Widerspruch der einzig Kompetente,
erledigt er die Thesen kunstgerecht.

Doch im Gewirr der Stimmen hört er eine,
bescheiden meldet diese sich zu Wort –
sie rührt von einem Mädchen, wie ich meine,
zu schön für einen faden Tagungsort.

Die Kleine äußert ihre kluge Meinung,
man applaudiert entsprechend, ist betört
zugleich von ihrer reizenden Erscheinung –
der Geist entgegnet gar nichts. Unerhört!

Dies eine Mal beliebt's ihm zu verzichten;
ein Raunen geht durchs Auditorium.
Und wirklich widersprach er ihr mitnichten –
man weiß bis heute nicht genau warum.

– – – –

Inzwischen wieder ganz im alten Gleise,
besucht er Diskussionen und besticht,
indem er JEDEM, auf bewährte Weise,
genüßlich formvollendet widerspricht.

IV. A Literary Mother Goose

FOLLOWED BY

The Tale of the 31 Cousins (Parlez-moi d'Amour)

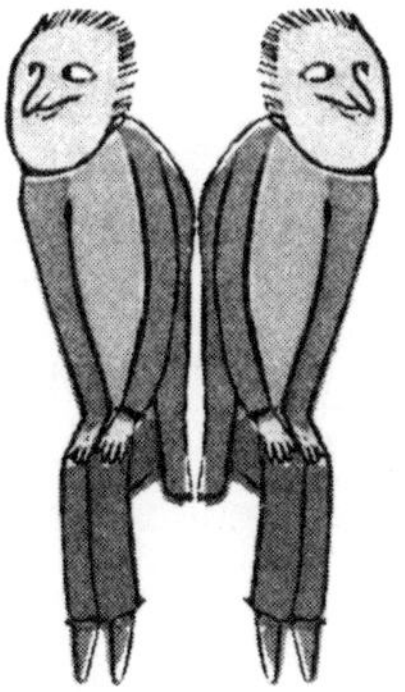

Social Contract

Jacques Rousseau
liked children so,
he begot
a biggish lot.

Living poorly,
they were surely
glad they had
a famous dad.

Belt-Tightening Waist-Watching

I tightened hers,
she tightened mine –
soon we got
to like it fine.

Others petted
or embraced –
we just watched
each other's waist.

Ill, Iller, Illest

I've never met a man so ill
but found not someone iller still;
not always is it he who shrillest
proclaims his illness who is illest.

Pie in a Fallen State

The filling
is willing,
the crust
is bust.

An Unsatisfactory Dish of Blueberries with Cream

The blueberries
are fewberries,
and the cream is
in extremis.

How my Wife and I Relate to Shakespeare

Where he enjoins me to be true
to mine own self,*) I like him most;
though I must say, I also do
enjoy the bit with Banquo's ghost.**)

Not so my wife: she is impressed
with Shylock, Romeo, and Lear –
reserving, as you may have guessed,
for Banquo nothing but a sneer.

*) Hamlet, Act I, Scene 3 **) Macbeth, of course.

Poles Apart

Boy in Bydgoszcz, girl in Gdansk –
licked before they start:
how indeed are they to meet,
being Poles apart?

"Make Hay While the Sun Shines"*)

Remembering the proverb bade
us go ahead and do it,
I picked a sunny day and made
some hay – and didn't rue it!

For, taking it to town, I sold
it quite without delay:
for silver coin and coin of gold –
and that, you know, ain't hay.

*) Monetaristic proverb dating back to the 16th century.
– *"Whan the sunne shynth make hey!"* (J. Heywood, 1546)

"Early to bed and early to rise
makes a man healthy, wealthy and wise."

How I Tried Heeding a Proverb – and it worked!

So I went to bed before
5 p.m., and rose at 4
(a.m.) – and to my surprise
I was healthy, wealthy, wise!

Noble Six Hundred

My father read Tennyson
after the venison,
I think from *Maud*
(the little bawd).
Whilst peeling quinces
he did *The Princess,*
or, too, was prone
to quote *Oenone.*
On sauce tartare
he *"crossed the bar".*

Walter Pater – Fanny Hill: A Little Known Episode

I remember Walter Pater
telling me he used to date her –
stopping when he found her weak
on some finer points of Greek.

(Pater, as an erudite
classicist, was never quite
able simply to enjoy
romping with the hoi polloi.)

(Note: Walter Horatio Pater, English essayist & classical scholar, was born in 1839; Fanny Hill is the name of a fictitious whore in a naughty book published 91 years earlier. So they probably never really met.)

Writers' Workshop

Elizabeth Barrett
sat in her garret,
madly scribbling away,
when in steps Browning,
darkly frowning,
bringing the curds and whey.

They ate their fill,
as poets will
when offered such cuisine:
they gobbled it down;
then, with less of a frown,
Bob licked the platter clean.

(Note: The poets Elizabeth Barrett and Robert Browning first met in 1845, and soon eloped to Italy, which brought them instant popularity and lasting stardom on stage and screen.

March Hare (on the Couch), Stating his Case to Dr. Freud

"I was formerly
quite normerly,
but am latterly
mad-hatterly."

Cousin Bridget

Cousin Bridget
set up home
with a midget
and a gnome.

Sick of such
she'd now much
rather try and
board a giant.

Felix Krull, Esq.

Felix Krull
went to Hull:
Jane Eyre
paid his fare;
Molly Bloom
paid his room;
Sister Carrie
made him tarry;
Fanny Hill
charged him nil;
Lorna Doone
made him swoon,
Hester Prynne,
live in sin. –
Little Dorrit
blamed them for it.

Whore with Robin-Hood-Complex

"I get rich on blokes who blame me,
but wish nonetheless to lay me;
then I go and really satis-
fy some poorer people gratis."

Tit for Tat

I'm not inclined to cavil at
a proper dose of tit for tat;
but would not also tat for tit
seem on occasion apposite?

How I Came to Found the Kames-Mutual-Profit-And-Bible-Society

While sojourning in Kames,
I read a King James
Bible and found
faith to abound –
a faith so rare, it
seemed proper to share it.

Now, stocking a lot
of such biblical ware,
I share it for what
the traffic will bear.

Pie in the Sky

A way will be discovered soon
to put one into orbit;
if it prove tasty, outer space
will gratefully absorb it.

"Smart Aleck"*)

This is how he got his label
(lesser reasons quite apart):
one, his name is really Alec,
two, he happens to be smart.

*) "Smart aleck": a cheaply clever person (Webster's); someone who is saucy and acts cocky (Pons); Besserwisser, Schlaumeier, Klugscheißer, wise guy, know-all, smart-arse (Rennert)

Take Up Axe-Grinding

I'm off to find
an axe to grind:
nothing relaxes
like grinding axes.

Witches' Sabbath

Secretaries spend a bleak,
mainly boring office week –
ergo desperately seek (and
sometimes find) a way-out weekend.

At Parties, When the Talk Turns to Strabo

Reading Strabo, Livy and
Pliny pays a dividend:
host and hostess welcome earthy
types who dig this type of worthy.

Rejoyceing in What We Have

Jimmy Joyce,
nearly blind,
has his voice
still, and mind:
quotes *Ulysses*
to his missis.
(Molly Bloom
makes her fume.)

Butler Yeats or Servant Trouble

(for William BUTLER Yeats)

Butler Yeats,
soon as look,
kissed the cook
and broke the plates.

So they fired
him and hired
Jimmy Joyce –
Milady's choice.

Pre-Raphaelite*) siblings at Dinner

Said Dante Rossetti,
wolfing spaghetti:
"I've never seen a
girl like Christina!"

Cracked she to Dante,
raising her Chianti:
"Nor has another
one such a brother!"

*) Pre-Raphaelites: An English art movement founded c.1850. Dante Gabriel and Christina Rosetti were prominent adherents, sharing an interest in pre-Renaissance art (and – so it seems – a liking for Italian food).

Walt Whitman-Digest

Of me I sing –
ding dong ding.
(To make my song longer,
I'd have to ding donger.)

White Whale of a Tale

(in memoriam Moby Dick)

My dad was born
off Cape Horn,
but kicked the bucket*)
near Nantucket.

In case you've not heard,
his famous last word
was: "Tell, will
you, Melville!"

*) Kick the bucket (slang, impolite): to die; kick off; bite the dust; croak; pass away. – *Don't say that George Washington "kicked off". Say that he "passed away".* (Pons, Idioms Dictionary, 1987)

An American Tragedy

Theodore Dreiser
was far the wiser,
but far the prettier
was Greenleaf Whittier.

Good Provider Brings Home the Bacon (Only)

Robbing brutely, he will take on
any passer-by with bacon;
then he sends his kids to beg
money for a scrambled egg.

Madame Récamier*)

Madame Récamier,
with plenty bon ton,
threw a swell soirée
in her nifty salon.
She telephoned
the demi-monde,
who liked it fine
to see recline
the famous belle.
But truth to tell:
they came to dine!
They liked her stew –
chacun à son goût.

*) French beauty, b. 1777, married a rich banker thrice her own age, entertained highbrows "in her nifty salon".

Pie-oneer

Before him there was no one
who undertook to throw one.

Caesar's Troops Cross the Polluted Rubicon

So they crossed it, though the stench
made the forward troopers blench.
Holding noses, all the rest
gloriously met the test.

Caesar, watching from the wings,
sniffed his valiant underlings,
proudly read the signs and knew:
"Pompey's definitely through."

The Linguist's Saturday Night

First he always tries to spot
harlots who are polyglot;
in the end he settles for
any ordinary whore.

What the Doctor Ordered

Soup, a pork chop, buttered peas,
deep-dish apple pie with cheese.
When he paid, I heard him stating
that the meal was nauseating.

Empedocles Down the Drain

He moved to the brink
of the kitchen sink,
prayed and leapt –
the brillo wept.

(Annual ritual re-enactment at Agrigentum in memory of the philosopher Empedocles who, after inventing a pre-soaped pad for scouring kettles, is said to have jumped into the flames of Mt. Aetna.)

Dante Interviewed at Broadway Opening of His New Comedy / Calls Show "Divine, But"

"*Heaven* seemed a trifle slow;
purgatory doubly so;
but the rest went very well:
my *inferno* looked like hell.

You will note, they changed the sequence;
mine, they told me, sort of weakens,
without making things seem truer,
the effect upon the viewer."

Shootenanny*)

Instead of his fiddle
he brought his gun,
aiming to riddle
the place for fun.

Many thought it
kind o'cute,
till they caught it
in the snoot.

Others thought it
quite a farce,
till they caught it
in the arse.

*) Hootenanny, US: an informal gathering with folk music. (OED)

Ugly Duckling into Swan?

My ugly duckling, lacking luck,
grew into an ugly duck.

It goes without Saying . . .

If indeed it goes that way, it
seems superfluous to say it.

Patrick Henry*) Comments on His Much-Quoted Request "Give Me Liberty or Give Me Death"

"'Tis no secret that I nursed
aspirations for the first;
knowing well, to get the latter
is a rather nasty matter.

And, you will agree, my bid
was successful: for I did
freely live for years, a noted
patriot – respected, quoted . . ."

*) Henry, Patrick, 1736–1799, American statesman & orator. Much quoted.

Paul Revere (1735–1818) – A Case Study in Longevity

Paul Revere
was a mere
83 when he died:
shows how healthy
was his stealthy
revolutionary ride.*)

*) undertaken on April 18, 1775; re-enacted by Harpo Marx in *Duck Soup* (1933)

The Real McCoy*)

A man by the name of McCoy
experienced predictable joy
when he heard he'd been labeled
"the real one" – the fabled,
unique and authentic McCoy.

*) The real thing; the genuine article. – *"This Bloody Mary sure hits the spot! It's the real McCoy."*

Byron Compared with Burns

It was his whim,
or even wont,
to try to swim
the Hellespont.
Did he indeed
at all succeed?

Burns was never
quite so clever,
but simply nice
to men and mice.

Odes with Milk – a Success Story

His mother fed him mother's milk,
his father read him Keats –
they must have loved the child indeed
to offer him such treats.

As, later on, he grew in wealth,
he frequently ascribed
this to the odes with milk which he
had as a babe imbibed.

The Life of Riley*)

A man who highly
regarded Riley,
wrote his Life,
then told his wife:
"If people read it,
we can lead it."

*) Lead the life of Riley (colloquial): have a carefree existence.
– *"With such small royalties, the poet Rennert could not expect to lead the life of Riley."*

Vacations

Taking a week off
is little to speak of;
taking a year off
is little you hear of.

Desire under the Elms

(Digest of the play by Eugene O'Neill)

Sometimes desire overwhelms
me while I'm walking under trees,
and when, of course, the trees are elms,
then it's desire under these.

Great Females of Literature Compared

I'd give all of Lassie for a
tiny glimpse of Ibsen's Nora;
but I'd surely rather wed a
collie than his dizzy Hedda.

Putting it in a Nut(s)shell
(Puns & Needles)

Epitaph for a Pre-eminent Bore

Foremost
Boremost.

(Shortest poem in the book.)

Blood is Thicker than Water

Is it thicker
than liquor?

Mary Shelley
At the mercy
of Percy.

United We Stand
This we do whenever it
proves impossible to sit.

Sing for my Supper?
In a crunch
I'll sing for lunch.

Limits of Growth
(for Dennis Meadowes)

Every midget with a zero
rate of growth is now a hero.

Religious Man of the Year
The guy they chose is
Holy Moses.

The Scribes' Union Elects its New Head
Bound to be
a Pharisee.

Face-Saving
There may be little grace
in saving such a face.

Pessimist's Unguent Date
I've got an appointment
with a fly in my ointment.

THE FINAL TORT

The final tort is
rigor mortis.

LINGUA FRANCA

Far too franca, I do fear,
to permit the kids to hear.

RENNERT THE RHYMER

Rennert the Rhymer
is an old-timer;
he'll rhyme away
your time of day
and rarely shun
Ye Ghastly Pun.

Good thing his verse
is fairly terse,
for some will bore us
enough to floor us.

THE CASE OF THE STAR-CROSSED ACRONYMS
or AN AFFAIR OF THE HEART

A Dame (DBE, DCB)
met an FLS, FRCP,
whom she fell for, I guess;
which occasioned distress
to her husband (CB, CBE)

DBE: Dame Commander of the Order of the British Empire
DCB: Dame Commander of the Order of the Bath
FLS: Fellow of the Linnean Society
FRCP: Fellow of the Royal College of Physicians
CB: Companion of the Order of the Bath
CBE: Commander of the Order of the British Empire

Family Saga
or The Tale of the 31 Cousins
(Count them!)

Cousin Daisy,
acting crazy;
Cousin Abbie
dresses shabby;
Cousin Bab
loves to gab;
Cousin Mary
looks so scary;
Cousin Jessie
looks like Nessie!
Cousin Corey,
bit too Tory;
Cousin Millie,
awful silly;
Cousin Lizzie,
pretty dizzy;
Cousin Mandy
steals the candy;
Cousin Ellie,
hooked on telly;
Cousin Terry
tipples sherry;
Cousin Lyn
ladles gin;
Cousin Jean
swigs poteen;
Cousin Vi
guzzles rye;
Cousin Hope
deals in dope;
Cousin Beulah,
in the cooler;

Cousin Gail,
out on bail;
Cousin Joy,
bit too coy;
Cousin Hester,
but a jester;
Cousin Mim,
wits too dim;
Cousin Merle –
not a girl!!
Cousin Jill
pays no bill;
Cousin Claire
will not share;
Cousin Dee-Dee
eats too greedy;
Cousin Bridget,
fuss and fidget;
Cousin Lou,
sniffing glue;
Cousin Di
slaps her thigh;
Cousin Susie
acts the floozie;
Cousin Sadie,
not a lady;
Cousin Charlotte,
near a harlot!
Cousin Nell –
kiss and tell.

V. Fafnir folgt dem Ruf nach Bayreuth
Be-Kind-to-Animals-Week

OR

Habitat, Care and Feeding of Paper Tigers

EIN VIERBEINER IM GEMEINDERAT?

Ein Gemeinderat in Schieren
geht daheim auf allen vieren.
(So besagen die Berichte
seines Kochs und dessen Nichte.)
Doch im Amt, wo dies verboten,
geht er auf den Hinterpfoten.

BE-KIND-TO-ANIMALS-WEEK:
LIONS IN THE STREET

Regrettably, I never meet
a hungry lion in the street.
Should I, however, I would straight-
away and gently lead him
where modern playwrights congregate,
and there I'd amply feed him.

VOGELSCHAU (MBH)
ODER DAS BLAUE VOM HIMMEL

Einäugig steht ein arrivierter
Augur und prüft des Himmels Blau;
er ist ein vielfach diplomierter
Augur und kennt das Blau genau.

Und was er sieht, entspricht den Gaben
des Sehers – welche Seltenheit:
es sind zwei kleine Unglücksraben
(nebst ihrem weiblichen Geleit).

Die Räblein ihrerseits, auf Touren,
mit Krächzen ihrer Wege ziehn –
erspähen plötzlich den Auguren
und: häufen Unglück, ach, auf ihn!

The Case of the Kindly Snake

I know a snake with kindness writ
upon the whole extent of it:
eight letters, neatly in a row,
bedecking it from head to toe
(the letters being – did you guess? –
k - i - n - d - n - e - s - s).

Fafnir folgt dem Ruf nach Bayreuth

„Ich legendäres altes Biest
hiermit nun dem bekunde,
der diese Zeilen freundlich liest:
Mich juckt meine alte Wunde.

Sie stammt von Siegfrieds Ungebühr
(tat mich mein Leben kosten) –
nun winkt in Bayreuth mir dafür
ein krisenfester Posten.“

Habitat, Care and Feeding of Paper Tigers

I had looked for one in many
countries, never finding any:
then I came across so fine a
specimen of one in China.

There, I found, to keep him in
proper shape and very thin,
he is fed (to his distress)
clippings from the Party press.

Despot Meeting Lions in the Street

(for three merry members of the Lions Club of Rome)

On seeing them, the despot frowned,
suspecting their intentions;
they were, however, simply bound
for one of their conventions.

Der Biber und Wir
(Kulinarische Notizen)

Die Menschen essen gerne Quiche,
der Biber nagt am Mittagstisch.

Die Tafelfreude, sieht man, eint
mitunter Mensch und Biber –
und doch ist dieser, wie mir scheint,
ein anderes Kaliber:

Da *uns* das feine Quiche behagt,
und ein Tiramisu,
hat *er* das dritte Bein benagt
und setzt dem vierten zu!

Gewiß, die *haute cuisine* verwöhnt
den Gaumen, doch ich wähne,
die Faser, der der Biber frönt,
ist besser für die Zähne.

Selbstverständnis eines Bibers

An Bäumen zu nagen, vermag er
so wohl wie kein sonstiger Nager.
Doch wär's ihm nicht lieber,
er wäre kein Biber
und hätte was Warmes auf Lager?
Mitnichten! eher scheint er stolz
auf jedes angenagte Holz.

Dies zeigt: Gewohntes hinterfragt man
nur selten (denn man ist's gewohnt).
Solange Bäume stehen, nagt man –
und denkt: Das hat sich sehr gelohnt!

Aus Rennerts *Zwei Jahre im Biberbau* (Brandstätter, Wien)

Die Raupe 'rum

Die Raupe 'rum
kreucht um und um –
ein Weg so lange,
ihr wird bange.

Was sie nicht weiß:
Es ist ein Kreis,
und keine Wende
im Gelände.

Noch manche Stunde
solcher Runde
bringt nicht die Kehre
der Misere.

So kreucht sie um,
die Raupe 'rum,
und endlich spricht:
„Führt's weiter nicht,
verbleibt zum Glück
der Weg zurück!"

Rat-Racing?
(from: "Journal of the Society for the Abolition of Myths")

I have never seen a rat
doing anything like that,
but have met with not a few
people who distinctly do.
Seeing it's a *human* game, it
quite behooves us to rename it.

Rabenväter

So benennt man unter Raben
die von männlichem Geschlecht –
selbstverständlich nur zurecht
solche, die auch Kinder haben.

Rabenkinder

So bezeichnen sich die Raben,
die noch ihre Eltern haben.

Centipede, Told to Put His Best Foot Forward

"Firstly, tell me *which* of these
feet of mine is best.
Then, supposing this were known,
what about the rest?

Each of the disqualified
ninety-nine will feel
second-best: and, feeling low,
start to drag his heel."

The Where-Wolf or Pretty Grimm

I know a *wolf* who knows not *where*
he gets his meals, nor does he care:
when he is ravenous, he eats
the first sweet little thing he meets,
or – rather than accept to fast –
seeks out a more mature repast.
Thus he has also eaten many
a granny – and was never any
the worse for such a very whim-
sical performance à la *Grimm.*

Sitting Duck

When no one watches,
he doth rise
and walk about
for exercise.

Bull, Sitting

Sitting bull,
his stomach full,
meant to sit
and think a bit.

Sit he knew
how to do,
but for thought
he managed aught.

Soon a cow
did appear,
for a pow-
wow, I fear.

Lied, bei der Kuhschur zu singen

Ich schere die Kühe,
das macht mir viel Mühe –
mein Arm schon erschlafft
vor Einbildungskraft!

Der Kühe sagt eine
mir dann, nur zum Scheine
sei Kuh sie, sie ahn' es:
als Auswuchs des Wahnes.

„Sei's drum", so die Kuh,
„scher du immer zu!
Bist du drauf erpicht,
so schert es mich nicht. –
Doch warte! – verflixt! – ich
spüre, du zwickst mich!"

Tomfoolery

Tomcat and tomfox
caroused with tomox.
Along came tomworm,
made all of them squirm.

Frühes Trauma des Vogels Roch

(aus: „Zeitschrift für Ornithologie“, 7/1892)

Der Vogel Roch,
was roch er doch
so früh, daß ihm noch bang ist?
Als er aus seinem Eilein kroch,
da roch sogleich der Vogel Roch
was da für ein Gestank ist.

Lied des Tausendfüsslers*)

Ich merke mit Befremden:
mir schlafen Füße ein –
so um zweidrittel werden
es jüngst gewesen sein!

Zu lange Märsche hätte
ich ihnen zugemutet,
so sagt man, und auch seien
sie mangelhaft durchblutet.

Mag sein. Es nahm die Sache
dann folgenden Verlauf:
dreihundertdreißig weckten
sechshundertsiebzig auf.

Die rieben sich die Äuglein
und schnürten sich die Schuh
und trabten, noch benommen,
auf neue Ziele zu.

*) Melodie: „Zeigt her eure Füße, zeigt her eure Schuh!“

Ein bemühtes Huhn

Ein Huhn aus dem Prätigau (Schweiz)
spräche gerne was wirklich Gescheits.
Es bemüht sich recht wacker,
doch bleibt es Gegacker.
Doch der Hahn meint, es hat seinen Reiz.

Der hohe Nord

(inspiriert von F. Nansens Buch *Durch Nacht und Eis*)

Durch Nacht und Eis
der Nordpol weiß
den Weg ins Warme
nicht, der Arme.

Sein Haus aus Schnee
in Polesnäh'
baut immerhin
ein Pinguin.

(Was kümmert's ihn,
den Pinguin,
daß süd er hat
sein Habitat.)

Ein Walroß schwimmt,
sofern das stimmt,
mit seiner Alten
gern im Kalten.

Ein Bär besinnt
sich auf sein Kind
und bringt ihm Aal
zum Abendmahl.

Ein Iltis pirscht –
die Scholle knirscht:
Die Beute bricht,
was sie verspricht.

Der Wolf erkiest
sich jedes Biest
mit Dankesehr
zum Frischverzehr.

Der Hai verzagt
nicht, sondern nagt,
mit leisem Fluch,
am Hungertuch.

Ein Eulchen strebt,
dieweil's noch lebt,
und voller Sehn-
sucht nach Athen.

Das Eis, es kracht
die halbe Nacht,
doch will mir scheinen,
stört es keinen.

MRS. WIGGS' CABBAGE PATCH

All had thought this dog too dead
to be barking through the night.
We had deemed the sun too red
to disintegrate on sight.

Those of us who were not cheering
used the interval for rest
(certainly not without fearing
that we might appear repressed).

Put all eggs in our platter,
count your chickens ere they hatch –
opportunities which matter
sprout on every cabbage patch.

Let us test the lady's virtue,
though she's really past her prime.
(Even masochists will hurt you,
given half a chance and time.)

MEDUSA (AND PERSEUS)

A Gorgon, who had what it takes,
sported tresses consisting of snakes.
With this kind of hairdo
she was certain to scare you.
(Just to think of it gives me the shakes!)

So, of course, she had no one to woo her.
Though thousands of citizens knew her
by hearsay, they took
good care not to look.
Till one hero said, "Dash it!", and slew her.

EIN EITLER PELIKAN

Ein Pelikan, wohnhaft in Dahnen,
ist stolz auf die Reihe der Ahnen.
Er bildet sich ein,
ein Adler zu sein.
Doch stammt er von zwei Pelikanen.

MÉNAGE À TROIS

Ein Floh verband sich (mésalliance!)
mit einer Laus und einer Wanze –
ménage à trois (es weiß die Bio-
logie noch nichts von solchem Trio).
Mir raubt das nächtliche Getue
im Bett die heißersehnte Ruhe.

– Vernehmt noch, was die Wanze spricht:
„Ich reime, mit Verlaub, mich nicht
auf mésalliance! Vom Dichten weiß ich
nicht viel zwar, doch die Dichter beiß ich."

VI. The Case of the Compulsive Rhymer

Endzeit gut, alles gut

Poetic License
or Brother, Can You Spare a Rhyme?

Versification is not what
it used to be. It was a lot
of fun well into Kipling's time
to versify with proper rhyme.
I know a man who does it still –
when no one watches him, he will
sit down in comfort, fully bent
on rhyming to his heart's content.

He uses paper, pen and ink
to write about the *bobolink,*
that strange and migratory fowl
which sometimes may be heard to howl
most rolickingly while it mates
in some of the United States.
If it should chance to fill the bill,
he writes about the *whippoorwill,*
a feathered friend who does nocturnal-
ly make a racket quite infernal.

Lest it be thought his stock of words
consists entirely of birds:
not so, he has amassed a store
of various and useful lore.
He uses "kith", quite often in
conjunction with the words "and kin";
he can distinguish "pit-a-pat"
from "pitch-and-toss" and "tit-for-tat".
He knows the difference between
a bloody king, a blooming queen;
a pot-pourri, a pompadour;
a paranoid, a paramour;
between Legree and Uncle Tom
(both being personages from
a book on cabins, which we owe,
I think, to Harriet Beecher Stowe).

He's keen on popery and can
tell Peter's pence from Peter Pan. –
Yet, he has paced the floor distraught-
ly, seeking rhymes on *juggernaut;*
and, finding aught, commenced to fuss
on what might go with *blunderbuss.*
But when he's happy, he'll invoke
some joke to rhyme with yoke or yolk,
then set himself to speculate
on being poet laureate. –
He prides himself on having found
some rhymes which would indeed astound
most poets of the English tongue.
In contexts hitherto unsung
he manifestly will outdo
the ardent, sensuous Carew
(whose year of death, as some opine,
was sixteen hundred thirty-nine;
while others think he was alive
to sixteen hundred forty-five).
But also Marvell, Gay and Swift
could not but marvel at his gift;
John Suckling would, and even so
would witty Pope und spooky Poe.
Of course, he'd utterly confound
Frost, Eliot, Yeats and Ezra Pound
('tis well these did not live to see
themselves surpassed so patently).

My friend will doubtlessly rhyme on
(a latter-day phenomenon)
till, with his very dying breath,
he notes the latter rhymes with *death.*
Nor may his passion quite abate
once he has passed the Pearly Gate:
with angels fluting, harping, chiming,
why should not one of them be rhyming?

Die Stadt am „Tag danach“ oder Der Wahlspruch zur Unzeit

Das Stadtsanierungsamt versprach
sich einiges vom „Tag danach“:
an diesem stand im Häusermeer
kein Haus mehr wie am „Tag vorher“.
Die City streckte alle viere
und hoffte, daß man sie saniere;
doch fehlte dazu der Beton,
auch Geld im Wiederaufbaufonds
(der Grund hierfür – ein ganz banaler:
Verdampfung aller Steuerzahler).
Das hat, wie eine Chronik lehrt,
ein kleiner „Schlagabtausch“ beschert.

Auch die historischen Gebäude
gereichten keinem mehr zur Freude;
kein Denkmal gab etwas zu denken
(die -pflege konnte man sich schenken).
Vom Laufsteg bis zum Boulevard
war das Verderben offenbar.
Das Münster und der Würstelstand
erwiesen sich als nur auf Sand
gebaut; das Freizeitareal
entpuppte sich als Jammertal.
Vom Hilton bis zum „Stillen Zecher“
glich's einem vollen Aschenbecher
(der Himmel sandte letzten Segen
in Form von einem Aschenregen).
Und also schien es ganz, als hole
der Teufel diese Metropole;
vom Pen-Club bis zum Tingeltangel
hob er das Leben aus der Angel.

Doch war in der verstrahlten Luft
ein Wahlspruch noch nicht ganz verpufft.
Er zog durch staubige Gefilde,
als führte er noch was im Schilde:
als müßten seine schlichten Thesen
nicht mit der Wählerschaft verwesen;
als wären sie – noch unvergessen –
auch *diesem* Zustand angemessen.

Im angewärmten Winde wehten
Gewebe vom Gemeinderäten,
ein kleiner Ungeist lässig spukte
auf einem Haufen Spaltprodukte,
zwei Funktionäre hatten pochen-
den Herzens sich darin verkrochen.
Der penetrante Grubendunst
erbrachte wenig Wählergunst,
er wirkte nämlich noch posthum
als sicheres Emetikum.

Die Katastrophenmedizin
floß übelriechend träg dahin,
darin – auch sie dahingerafft –
ein kleiner Rest der Ärzteschaft;
fünf Lehrer flossen mit im Brei,
die Schüler hatten heute frei.

Geschlossen waren die Spelunken,
die Nobeltreffs im Kot versunken,
vor einem schlürften Nagetiere
aus Holland importierte Biere.
Im Umfeld städtischer Museen
war nirgendwo ein Bild zu sehen,
doch roch ein frischer Klumpen Kleister
nach den Produkten alter Meister.

Geschmolzen waren die Bordelle,
geborsten auch die Planungsstelle
für dreißig neue Bankfilialen
samt Werbespots und Machtzentralen.
Verknistert war die EDV,
verronnen waren „Tagesschau",
das „Wort zum Sonntag", „Zeit im Bild" –
sie hatten keinen Hitzeschild.
Die „Dallas"-Sippe hatte mitten
in einer Bosheit ausgelitten.
Schier nichts war in der Flimmerkiste
und keiner da, der es vermißte.
Es stand auch nichts mehr in der Zeitung
von Brennstoffwiederaufbereitung.

Erledigt waren kleine Sparer,
Kapitalisten, Autofahrer,
der Sextourismus, Impotenzen,
Hostessen, graue Eminenzen,
der Wald, die Luftverschmutzungsnormen,
die Mode, Liturgiereformen,
die Kaufkraft, die Investitionen,
die Opfer ihrer Illusionen,
Polygamie, der Status quo,
das Zölibat, der Sparefroh,
Tabakregie und Raucherbein,
der alte Fritz, die Wacht am Rhein,
die Supermächte, Pufferstaaten,
das „Heitere Beruferaten".

Zusammen landeten im Eimer
der Wallenstein, die Pappenheimer,
die Troglodyten, Veteranen
des kalten Krieges, die Schamanen,
ein Nihilist, zwei Pietisten,
drei durchtrainierte Masochisten,

die Mediensprecher, Bauernbund,
der Überbau, der Untergrund,
ein Nestbeschmutzer, Mandatare,
ein Disko-Freak, drei Jubelpaare,
gekrönte Häupter und Lemuren,
die Hauptmannstöchter und die Huren.
Und niemand da, dem's mißbehagte,
und keiner, der es hinterfragte.

Zerbrochen waren Post und Knast
und der Versicherungspalast.
(Des Unterganges Schattenseite:
die generelle Haftungspleite.
Auch deckte keinerlei Polizze
Enteignungen durch Siedehitze;
und jeder Anspruch war erloschen,
vom Pfandbrief bis zum Krisengroschen.
Allüberall im Angesicht
des Endes übte man Verzicht;
die Welt blieb gerne unentschädigt,
sie hatte sich von selbst erledigt.)

Verschwunden die Entrepreneure,
die Eiertänzer, Kirchenchöre,
die Pazifisten und das Heer,
die Zebrastreifen, der Verkehr,
Agnostiker und Apostaten,
drei tiefe Bässe, vier Kastraten,
Gerüchteküchen, Gänsestopfer,
die Gründerväter, Sprücheklopfer,
der schwarze Peter, Alma mater,
ein Utopist, ein obligater
Betriebsratsobmannstellvertreter,
ein Macher und ein Wundertäter,
Souffleure, Jodler, Fetischisten,
die Pfuscher, die Professionisten,

die Lobbyisten, Dunkelmänner,
acht V.I.P.s, neun Sushi-Kenner,
ein Hedonist, zwei Puritaner,
ein Schreiberling, ein Krausianer,
die Filmemacher, Cineasten,
die Rocky-Horror-Enthusiasten,
die Kommunarden, Hottentotten,
die süßen Mädel, die Kokotten,
die Texter und die Liedermacher,
der Papst und seine Widersacher
(drei bibelfeste Drewermänner),
elf Sissy-Bücher (Dauerbrenner).
Es waren außerdem verschollen
diverse Schöpfer-aus-dem-Vollen.
(Kein „Szene"-Kenner, notabene,
beweinte den Verlust der Szene.)

Verloren waren die Prozesse.
Vergangen war das Interesse
an Pornostreifen, „freier Fahrt",
an Punkerlook und Rauschebart,
an Friesenwitzen, „Derrick" und
am Orbitalverkehrsverbund;
an Unisex und saurem Regen,
Verkabelung, Vergeltungsschlägen,
an Bodybuilding, Opernball,
an Futter voller Schwermetall.
Von heut' auf morgen nicht mehr „in"
war auch die Frage nach dem Sinn.
Der Urknall war nicht mehr gefragt
(und bis auf weiteres vertagt.)

Das Horoskop, Demoskopie
erweckten keine Nostalgie.
(Von Meinungsforschern gab es keinen,
der wissen wollte, was wir meinen.)
Am Kiosk prangte kein Gesäß,
denn dies war nicht mehr zeitgemäß.

Auch die Aerobic mußte passen –
das Fieber hatte nachgelassen.
Der Lottosechser war kein Ziel mehr,
das Köpferollen gab nicht viel her.
Sogar die Dichter gaben Frieden
und lasen nicht in Alten Schmieden.
Ein Tonangeber – dies das Schöne –
hielt dicht und sparte sich die Töne.

Und keiner glaubte an Atome,
an schwarze Löcher, Karzinome,
an Trümmerfrauen, an den GAU
(die Trümmer gab's, doch keine Frau).
Und nichts erhitzte die Gemüter;
die Leute wirkten abgebrühter.
Der Zeugungstrieb war abgestumpft,
das Wachstum unter Null geschrumpft,
und nicht die kleinste Spur verblieb
vom Lustgewinn, vom Todestrieb.
Und wo man hinsah – weit und breit:
bewältigte Vergangenheit!

Zerstoben auch der Magistrat,
der ehedem um Gelder bat
(von seinen Mühen kündet noch
ein wahrhaft bodenloses Loch).
Drei Ratten sammelten Furage
vom Tisch der letzten Vernissage,
ein Ungeziefer suchte Schutz
im warmen Konsumentenschmutz.

Von Menschen aber gab es nur
in der Erinn'rung eine Spur;
doch wen erinnert wer an was
nach einem solchen Aderlaß?
Es gab zu viele Tote, und
die litten an Gedächtnisschwund.

So trat bei der erwähnten Lage
nur wenig Pietät zutage,
und kam es denn, am „Tag danach“,
daß es der Stadt an Mut gebrach.
Der Wahlspruch war sich seiner Sache
nicht sicher – ob er weitermache? –
und endlich sprach: „Genug gequält!
ich werde diesmal nicht gewählt.“

Lustgewinn or Thinly Grinned the Asteroid

Thinly grinned the asteroid
at the witches' incantation.
Quoting Beelzebub and Freud
in a longish lamentation,

mingling moans and locomotion
striking viewers as propitious,
they were stirring up a potion
promising to be delicious.

Stamping, snorting, noses twitching,
sweating, eyes ablaze with zeal,
they exuded a bewitching,
if elusive, sex appeal.

Orphic beeps, a fit of choking,
sudden shrieks, a plaintive question –
answered by a burp evoking
fears of cosmic indigestion.

Sickly paled the asteroid
at such daunting sight and din,
then bestrode the outer void,
seeking other *Lustgewinn.*

Die Deutsche Bibliothek – CIP-Einheitsaufnahme

Rennert, Erwin:
Wirrwarrverse : ein Nonsens-Almanach in
deutsch und englisch / Erwin Rennert. – Wien : Brandstätter,
1996
ISBN 3-85447-595-0
NE: Rennert, Erwin: Wirrwarrverse

1. Auflage

Die graphische Gestaltung des Werkes sowie der Entwurf des
Schutzumschlags – mit einer Zeichnung von Edward Lear –
stammen von Christian Brandstätter.
Das Lektorat besorgte Gabriela Hamböck,
technische Herstellung Franz Hanns.
Satz und Reproduktion der Vignetten erfolgten
bei Zehetner Ges. m. b. H. in Oberrohrbach.
Gesetzt wurde aus der Adobe Garamond, 11,5 auf 11,5 Punkt.
Das Werk wurde beim Wiener Verlag in Himberg
gedruckt und gebunden.

ISBN 3-85447-595-0

Christian Brandstätter Verlagsgesellschaft m b. H.
A-1080 Wien, Wickenburggasse 26, Telephon (0043-1) 408 38 14

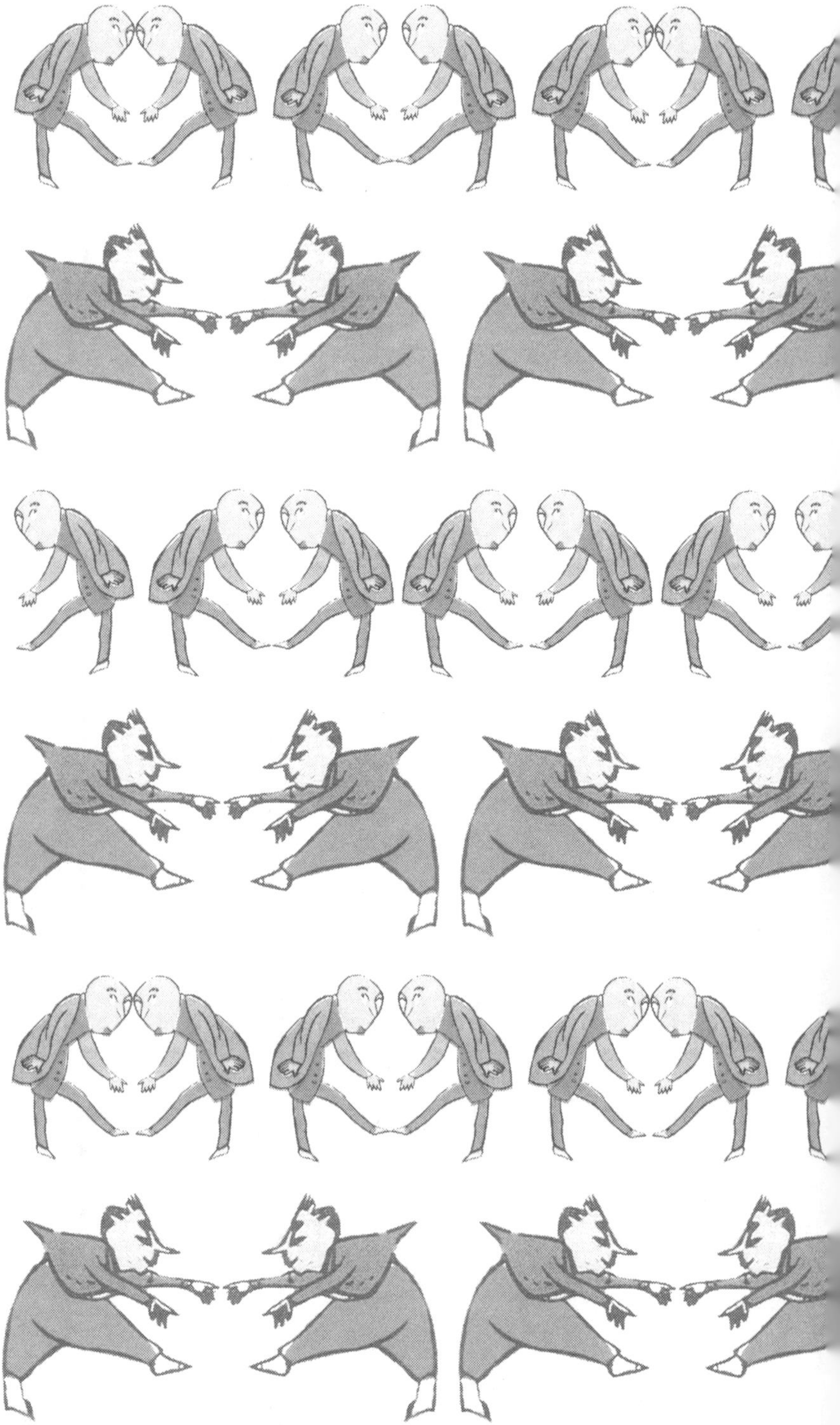